いちどきり の おくりもの

さく・え　すぎうらえいか

ここは　なんきょく。
ペンギンたちは　こおりの　うえで　たまごを　うみます。
ママが　うんだ　たまごを　あたためるのは　パパの　やくめ。
けれど…

こくり、こくり、いねむりをして
たまごが　こおりの　うえに　ころころころ…
「たいへん！　あかちゃんが　こごえちゃうわ！」
そらから　みていた　おつきさまは
ありったけの　ひかりを　たまごに　そそぎました。

その　よくあさのこと──

「おっと！ うっかり　ねてしまった！！
おや？ たまごが　ひかってる！
おつきさまみたいだ」
パパが　おそるおそる
たまごに　ふれると…
ぱかっ！
あかちゃんが　でてきました。
おとこのこです。

「おお、よかった！
やあ、パパだよ、ぼうや」
「ピッ…」
「ありゃりゃ？ げんきがないぞ。
ほら、もっと　ないてごらん」
「ピィ…」
それでも　ペンギンのこは
ちいさく　ないただけ。

ほかのこと　くらべても　よわよわしく

どこか　ぼうっとしているので

みんなに　からかわれました。

「ぼくなんて きっと
うまれてこなければ よかったんだ」
よる、ペンギンのこは
ひとりで わあわあ なきました。
すると とおくのほうで
こえがしました。
「そんなことないわ、ぼうや」
「だ、だあれ？」

「ここよ。わたし。おつきさま」
おつきさまは　ひかりの　てを
そうっと　のばして
ペンギンのこを　つつみこみました。
「さあ、なみだを　ふいて。
こっちへ　いらっしゃい」

ふわあっ
「すごい！ ぼく、とんでる！」

「よく　きたわね、ぼうや。
わたしの　うえで　やすんでいいよ」
おつきさまの　やさしい　まなざしに
ペンギンのこは　おもわず　うっとり。

おつきさまは　ペンギンのこが
うまれる　まえの　よるのことを
はなしてくれました。

「うわあ、ぼく　あんなに　とおくから　きたんだ。
おつきさま、あのなかから　よく　ぼくの　たまごを
みつけたね」
「ふふふ。ここからでも　よぉく　きこえたわ。
ぼうやが　うまれたいって
たまごの　なかで　いっているのがね」
「ぼく　うまれたがってたんだ…」

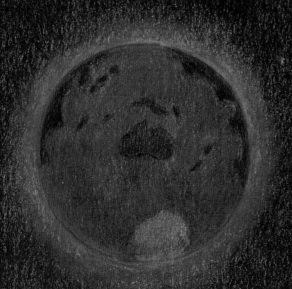

「あっ、ながれぼし！」

「つーかまえた！」 「すごいや！」

おつきさまの　まわりを
びゅーん、ぐるり。
「ぼくのが　いちばん　はやいぞ！
やっほー！」

あそびつかれると
おつきさまは　おはなしをしてくれました。
とおい　ほしたちから　つたわる
ふしぎで　ゆめのような　おはなし…
ずうっと　きいていたいと
ペンギンのこは　おもいました。
けれど…

「そろそろ　おひさまが　かおをだすわ。
さあ、もう　かえりなさい」
「ぼく…かえるの　いや！
おつきさまと　ずっと　いっしょにいる！」
「それは　できないのよ。
そのかわり　このいしを　どうぞ。
これに　ねがえば　また　あえるわ。
でもね、　これは　ひとつしかないの。
つかえるのは　たった　いちどきり。
だから　よぉく　かんがえて
つかってちょうだいね」

おつきさまに　さようならを　いって
ペンギンのこは　ながれぼしに　のって　かえってきました。
ながれぼしは　すぐに　きえてしまい、
のこったのは　おつきさま　そっくりの　ちいさな　いしだけ。
「だれにも　みつからないように
　この　こおりのやまの　ねもとに　うめておこう」

それからも　ペンギンのこは
あの　こおりのやまの　うえで　なんども　なきました。
やさしかった　おつきさまが　こいしくて
なんども　いしを　つかいたくなりました。
けれど　そのたび　ペンギンのこは　おもったのです。

「いちどきり…、たった　いちどきりなんだ。
きっと　それは　いまより　もっと　つらいときに
とっておくほうが　いいってことだよね」

そうして　なみだを　ぬぐっては
よぞらを　あおぎみるのでした。

それから　つきひは　すぎてゆき──

ペンギンのこは
おとなの　ペンギンになり…

およめさんと　こどもに　めぐまれました。
さむい　さむい　なんきょくでの　こそだては
とっても　たいへん。
それでも　あたたかい　かぞくの　ぬくもりに
ペンギンは　しあわせいっぱいでした。

そうして　いつしか　おつきさまの　いしを
おもいだすことは　なくなっていったのです…

それから　また　ずいぶん　ときが　ながれました。
おじいさんになった　ペンギンは　また　ひとりぼっち。

あるよる　こおりのやまの　ねもとで
なにかが　ひかっているのを　みつけました。
「おや…。あれは　もしや…」

「そうそう。おつきさまに　もらって　すぐ
ここに　うめたんだったなあ…」
ペンギンの　むねは　なつかしさで
あつく　なりました。

「ああ、ぼくは　もう
こんなに　としを　とってしまった。
おつきさま、それでも　とべるかな…」

すると　いしは　それに
こたえるかのように
きらきらと　まぶしく　ひかりはじめました。
ひかりは　ペンギンを
やわらかく　つつみこみ──

ペンギンは　よぞらに
たびだったのです。

Gift for one-time use
Written and illustrated by Sugiura Eika

Here at Antarctica,
penguins are laying eggs on ice.
Mommy penguins lay eggs, and Daddy penguins keep them warm.
However…

One day, daddy penguin is nodding off,
and his egg starts rolling on ice…
"Oh, no! Baby in the egg must be freezing!"
From the sky far above, the big Moon notices it
and pours all of her light over the egg.
The next morning—

"Oh no! I fell asleep!
Why? The egg is glowing!
It's shining like the moon."
When Daddy penguin timidly touches the egg…
Pop!
Baby penguin came out from inside the egg. It's a boy!
"Awww, my baby!
I'm your daddy, my baby boy!"
"P…pip…"
"Aghhh…sounds kind of weak.
Baby boy, it's okay. You can be louder."
"C…cheep…"
But the baby penguin just whispers a bit.

He is always weaker than his friends (Kerchoo--)
and always flabby; (Plop!)
so everyone picks on him. (Na-nana-na-na!)
"Why I am like this?
Maybe I shouldn't have been born in this world."
Baby penguin is sobbing in the night by himself.
Suddenly, he hears someone talking to him from far away.
"Oh, baby, that's not true."
"What? Who is it?"

"Up here. It's me, the Moon."
The Moon gently extends her glowing hands down
and wraps him softly with her light.
"Baby, wipe your eyes and come over here."

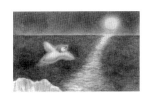

"Wow!!! I am flying!!"

"I'm so happy to have you here, baby.
Why don't you lay down right here?"
Baby penguin's heart is melted by her embracing gaze.
The Moon shares the story of the night before he was born.

"Wow, I came from there? So far away!
How could you find me in that little egg from way over here?"
"(Chuckled) I could hear you clearly
inside that little egg saying, 'I can't wait to come out'"
"Was I saying that…?"

"Woah! Shooting stars!"
"I got them!" "Yaaay!"
Swoosh! Hopping on a star, he is flying around the Moon.
"Look! My star is faster! Whoo-hoo!"

When Baby penguin gets tired, the Moon shares many stories,
mysterious and fantastic stories from distant stars…
Baby penguin wishes the stories would last forever.
Then…

"Soon the Sun will be coming up. It's time for you to go home."
"No…I don't want to go back there! I want to stay with you!"
"You can't. Do you hear me? But you can have this stone.
You can come here again when you make a wish on this.
But, listen, this is the only one you will have,
and only one wish can be granted.
That is why you need to think carefully about when you want to use it."

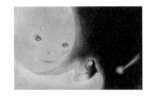

Baby penguin says good-bye to the Moon
and comes back home, riding on a shooting star.
As soon as he lands, the star disappears,
and he is holding the tiny stone, glowing like the Moon, in his hand.
"I'm hiding it at the bottom of this iceberg so that no one will find it."

Many times, Baby penguin climbs to the top of the iceberg
when he wants to cry.
He misses the kind Moon so much and thinks of using the glowing stone,
but he always hesitates to do so because…
"Only one time…I can use it only one time to make the wish;
so I have to save it for when I have the hardest time.
Isn't that right, Moon?"
Then, he wipes his tears and looks up to the dark sky.
Years go by…

Baby penguin is not a baby anymore and grows into an adult penguin.
Now he has a family with his wife and a baby of his own.
It is so harshly cold in Antarctica, and it is not easy to raise a child.
And, yet, he is happily living there and embracing his family dearly.
Gradually, he stops thinking of the tiny stone
the Moon gave him…

Many more years go by.
Now he is an old penguin, and he is living by himself.
One night, at the bottom of an iceberg, he sees something glowing.
"Wait…could that be…maybe…"

"That's right. I hid it here
when I came back from the Moon!"
His heart is filled with warm feelings, remembering the experience.
"Oh, my…I am so old now.
Dear Moon, can I still fly up to come see you…?"
Soon, the tiny stone starts shining brightly, as if replying to his wish.
The bright light gently embraces the old penguin,
and…

He flies high into the dark sky to see the Moon again.

すぎうらえいか

1986 年、東京都に生まれる。絵本作家。
日本女子大学家政学部児童学科にて絵本について学び、
2015 年より絵本制作を開始。
きむらゆういち氏主宰「ゆうゆう絵本講座」に参加。
2016 年、日本児童文学者協会「あなたのとなりにある不思議」入選。
「にじ色のえほんとおはなし展」（積雲画廊）、
「えほん展」（ミレージャギャラリー）、
「カラフル自由研究〜絵本編〜」（ギャラリー ちいさなつき）など出展多数。
うさぎが大好きで、ペンギンも好き。

いちどきりのおくりもの

2019 年 11 月 14 日　第 1 刷発行

著者　　　　　　すぎうらえいか　©Eika Sugiura 2019
発行者　　　　　落合加依子
発行所　　　　　小鳥書房
〒186-0003 東京都国立市富士見台 1-8-15
電話　070-1500-1568（代表）

編集　　　　　　落合加依子、中山京子
編集協力　　　　あらやはるのふ、水石紗穂、織田祥代、千野龍也、横田和子
装丁・デザイン　すぎうらえいか
英訳　　　　　　眞野裕美、Diana C Nadas
印刷・製本　　　シナノ書籍印刷株式会社

Printed in Japan
ISBN 978-4-908582-04-2